PANDA PANIC

Jamie Rix

Illustrated by
Sam Hearn

HarperCollins *Children's Books*

First published in Great Britain by
HarperCollins *Children's Books* 2012
HarperCollins *Children's Books* is a division of
HarperCollins*Publishers* Ltd, 77-85 Fulham Palace Road,
Hammersmith, London W6 8JB

Visit us on the web at
www.harpercollins.co.uk

1

ISBN 978-0-00-746768-6

Printed and bound in England by Clays Ltd, St Ives plc

For Buster. An awesome dog who pants
like a panda.

CHAPTER ONE

L ying on her back, with her legs crossed at a jaunty angle, Mao Mao stripped the bamboo shoot with her teeth, then using the soggy stump as a pointing stick, waved it in front of her face.

"Look," she said, munching methodically

on the woody pulp in her mouth. "There's a giant panda up there in the sky."

Her daughter An, who was lying by her side and chewing on her own stick of bamboo, raised her eyes to look.

"And it's being chased by a golden monkey," she said without surprise, swallowing what was left in her mouth before taking another bite.

"I could watch clouds all day," said her mother. "They make such interesting shapes. And they're so quiet, so respectful. When you're resting, listening to a sea of green bamboo growing, the last thing you want is a noisy interruption."

"I agree," said An. "Nobody likes a

screaming wind or a crashing wave. Here on the grassy slopes of Mount Tranquil we prefer whispering clouds and the chuckle of a gentle stream."

"You're a girl after my own heart," sighed Mao Mao, brushing a fly off the tip of her black-and-white nose. And with that, mother and daughter snuggled down into the soft bed of rhododendron leaves and prepared themselves for another tiring day of doing nothing.

Then suddenly, from the other side of the bamboo hedge, there was a terrifying scream. The very earth they were lying on seemed to rattle and shake, families of frightened grandala birds took flight and, sitting bolt upright, An choked on her mouthful of pulp. A second scream accompanied by the thundering thump of heavy paw-steps made Mao Mao's eyes snap open.

"What on earth!" she cried, sitting up and shaking the sleep out of her head by boxing her ears with the palms of her paws. Deep in a fuzzy recess of her brain a motherly instinct was sounding a warning that the scream belonged to her only son – An's twin brother, Ping. But before she could shout at him to keep the noise down, the bamboo hedge to her right was flattened by a young

12

panda cub, who tumbled through it and landed with a distinct lack of respect on her belly. It knocked the wind out of her, not to mention the chewed bamboo in her mouth, which pinged off Ping's ear like a bottle top.

Still panting, Ping flipped over and stood up on his mother's round stomach as if she was nothing more than a grassy knoll.

"Run for your lives!" he yelled, grabbing the stick of bamboo out of his sister's mouth and tugging at her paw to drag her to her feet. "Your lives are in danger!"

An refused to budge and snatched the stick of bamboo back.

"*Don't just lie there!*" yelled Ping. "Mummy, please! Get up! Stir yourself!"

"How can I," she said calmly, "when there's somebody *standing* on me?"

Ping jumped down and prodded his mother's arm.

"There are poachers right behind me," he cried urgently. "They've got literally millions of panda hides slung across their shoulders."

"Millions?" she said, raising her eyebrows.

"Well, seven or eight," admitted Ping. "But there is a look of killing in their eyes. If you don't want to end up as a rug, follow me now!"

But Ping's mother was unmoved. She simply snapped off another stick of bamboo from the hedge and resumed her methodical chewing. Ping had never seen such indifference to danger and redoubled his efforts.

"What's the matter with you two?" he hollered. "Do you want to die?"

Mao Mao leant forward and biffed Ping round the ear.

"Ow!" he cried. "What was that for?"

"You've interrupted my meal," said his mother. "Not to mention the lovely peace and quiet."

"But there are poachers," Ping said half-heartedly. Even he appeared to be losing interest in the life-or-death news.

"If there are poachers," his mother said evenly, "then I'm a panda from another planet; and I'm *not*, as you very well know, Ping. I am a panda from the Wolagong Nature Reserve, who sits in this clearing in the Serene Forest for fourteen hours a day eating bamboo – a lifestyle, incidentally, which suits me very well, but which, it would appear, does not appeal to you."

"It's boring," said Ping. "And why does nobody ever believe a word I say?"

"Because your lying stinks worse than golden monkey poo," sniggered his sister, sticking out her tongue at him. "And it's easy-peasy to spot when you're lying because your mouth curls up like an ancient lychee into a snooty, 'Aren't-I-so-clever' smirk."

"You're not helping, An," said Mao Mao, before turning her disapproving gaze back to her son. "How many times do I have to tell you, Ping, to stop making up stories."

"There's nothing else to do around here," he protested.

"You could eat bamboo," she said.

"Oh, whoop-di-do!" Ping cheered sarcastically. "I can eat bamboo and poo forty-seven times a day!"

"There's no need to be rude," said his mother. "Giant pandas have lived this way for thousands of years."

"Well, maybe it's time for a change," suggested Ping. "Maybe I wasn't born to pose for the endless stream of visitors who pass by every day with their cameras. *Maybe* I am destined to be the first panda in the history of Wolagong who was born to lead a life of excitement and adventure! I have been speaking to my friend Hui and—"

An interrupted him.

"Hui is just a birdbrain," she said dismissively. "I don't believe anything he says either."

"Hui is a grandala bird, who travels the world and knows everything," Ping corrected her. "And he says that the world is full of interesting animals just waiting to meet me."

His mother lay back down and contemplated the sky.

"*It is enough that water is wet,*" she said

meaningfully. *"It cannot also be fire."*

Ping sighed. His mother was fond of her irritating little sayings. She had a habit of slipping them into a conversation when she wanted the conversation to stop. Deep down Ping knew that she was right. A panda was a panda and he shouldn't try to be something else. But that didn't mean he couldn't dream, did it?

Moving away from his mother and sister, Ping sat down out of their sight and picked up a handful of the bamboo stalks that he'd knocked over earlier when he'd tumbled through the hedge. He was just taking his first bite when there was a scampering and a chattering behind him, and before he could say, 'What on Wolagong!' he was surrounded by an excitable troop of golden monkeys.

"What do you want?" he said, knowing full well what the monkeys wanted – what monkeys *always* wanted. To tease him. Pandas are quiet, contemplative creatures that like to think deeply, but golden monkeys are noisy chatterboxes interested only in tittle-tattle and gossip. In short, monkeys are trouble.

"Hello, Ping," mocked their leader, Choo. "Having another busy day?"

The other monkeys sniggered at their leader's brilliant wit.

"Been eating lots of bamboo, have you?

Had a few poos? Posed for some cameras?"

The sniggering increased to such a volume that Ping felt the need to defend himself.

"Actually, yes," he said, bigging himself up. "I have had an extremely busy day, thank you, Choo. Some might even say a heroic day!"

The monkeys gasped and exchanged looks of mock admiration.

"I saw one of the visitors trying to steal a golden pheasant," Ping continued, "and when I realised that there wasn't time to call a ranger and that I was the bird's only hope, I took a deep breath and grabbed on to a creeper and swung through the trees like a stealthy shadow until I was hanging over the top of the villainous visitor. I must have been at least ten metres above his head. Probably more. Anyway, without any thought for my own safety, I let go of the creeper and bravely dropped on to his head, driving the visitor into the ground like a fence post. And after he'd pulled himself out and run away screaming, the golden pheasant put its wing on my shoulder and said, 'Truly, Ping, you are a great hero. You have saved my life when nobody else could. And if we had a king here in the Wolagong Nature Reserve, you can bet that I'd put you up for the job because you are the best.' And that's how

I've spent my day!"

At the very least Ping was expecting a pat on the back accompanied by a shame-faced apology, but instead, when he turned around, the monkeys were rolling on the ground clutching their bellies and laughing.

"You are such a fibber!" Choo screamed, leaping up into a tree and swinging back into the forest. "The lousiest liar in Wolagong."

In a trice the other monkeys followed their leader into the trees and Ping was suddenly alone with only the echoes of their cruel laughter to keep him company.

The young panda cub slumped to
the ground and rested his chin in his paw
as he mulled over his life.

"I hate it when the monkeys are right,"
he told himself. "Being a panda IS really
dull."

He felt his mother's paw stroke the top of his head.

"*Do not fear going forward slowly. Fear only standing still,*" she said, giving his shoulder a squeeze.

"Actually there's another saying that's much more appropriate," Ping said.

"Really?" she replied. "I'd love to hear it."

"*Do not fear going forward looking like a doodoo-headed ninnyhammer. Fear only being a doodoo-headed ninnyhammer,*" he said.

"And is that what you think you are?" his mother asked. "A doodoo-headed ninnyhammer?"

Ping turned and stared at her through black-ringed eyes and couldn't find a way of saying 'Yes' without sounding sorry for himself. Instead he said, "I'm going to bed," and trotted away with his tiny tail between his legs.

But he couldn't sleep.

As he tossed and turned on his bed of rhododendron leaves, the long, cold night carved out the truth. His life was standing still. If he didn't do something exciting soon, he would almost certainly turn into a stone.

But, that night, as luck would have it, his wish for excitement was granted.

CHAPTER TWO

Ping must have fallen asleep in the end because the next thing he remembered was being woken up by the sound of a twig snapping nearby.

Flashing a look across the clearing, he was alarmed to see that both his mother and sister were asleep in their beds. So it wasn't them he could hear creeping up on him... in the dead of night... breathing. He could definitely hear breathing. The low rumble of a big cat's purr.

Ping sat up, his heart pounding like the rat-tat-tat of a Chinese woodpecker. A big cat could only mean one thing.

A snow leopard! A gizzard-guzzling, meat-munching, sinew-slashing snow leopard! And snow leopards ate panda cubs for breakfast every day of the week!

Well, *not* today. Not if Ping had anything to do with it...

He rolled out of bed as silently as a slithering moon-shadow and sprang to his feet, pushing himself up on to the very tips of his tippy-toes. Then treading as delicately as a mountain shrew, he pushed his way into the field of bamboo and circled round to his right.

His plan was simple. He would creep up behind the snow leopard and take it by surprise. Brilliant. What was it his mother always said? *"There is nothing to fear except fear itself."* Ping wasn't scared. Far from it. He was pumped up to his eyeballs with courage. Then, suddenly, there in front of him, he saw his target: a black-and-white-spotted shape flickering through gaps in the bamboo screen and slinking towards the clearing where his mother and sister were asleep. They would be breakfast unless Ping could save them.

Standing on his back legs, he stretched up and slid a creeper off the branch above his head, all the while keeping his eyes fixed on his target. It was now or never…

Ping pounced!

With a terrifying scream designed to befuddle the snow leopard's senses, and a cry of, "Claws off my mummy!", Ping leapt out of the night sky, landed on the back of the animal, and keeping hold of the two ends of the creeper, forced the middle section in between the stalker's jaws.

Pulling on the creeper like a rein, he tugged the snow leopard sharply to its

left, dug his heels into its sides, then rode
the beast into the bamboo forest while his
mother and sister slept on… safe and –
more importantly – saved!

Only when Ping reached the top of

a mighty waterfall did he and the snow leopard part company. As the big cat tumbled into the deep pool at the bottom of the fall, Ping, who was standing on an overhanging rock at the top, dusted his paws, shaded his eyes and looked out towards the wide horizon with all the puff and swagger of a mighty hero.

And then he woke up.

His sister was staring down at him, giggling.

"What have you just been doing?" she asked. "You were shouting something about *saving your mummy*, then punching the air with your paws and bouncing your bottom up and down on the ground as if you were riding a lying-down horse."

Ping sat up, confused to find himself back in his bed.

"Oh," he said disappointedly. "I was dreaming."

"I bet you were fighting a snow leopard," she sniggered, as if such a thing could *never* happen.

"I might have been," said Ping indignantly. He was feeling a little foolish now. One moment he was *Ping the Leopard Slayer*; the next he was just plain old unexciting Ping again.

"I bet you were winning too," added An.

"Why?"

"Because it was a dream, and boys who

can't fight are always brilliant fighters in their dreams."

What annoyed Ping about his sister was that she was such a know-all, who had a knack of knowing everything about everyone, even when she hadn't been told a thing.

"I jolly well *can* fight," he said unconvincingly.

"No, you can't," she laughed. "In real life, you couldn't even fight a fly. Well, you could, but you'd lose."

"I could beat *you!*" he said, rising to the challenge.

"No, you couldn't," she said, "because I am a lady and I wouldn't *let* you fight me."

"And I am a man and wouldn't listen to you," he retorted.

"If you were a man, you would do what a lady said," she replied primly.

"You're not a lady," he scoffed, "you're my sister, so that doesn't count."

"Actually, it counts *more*."

"No, it doesn't. When have you *ever* said anything remotely interesting that I would want to listen to? Never! That's when."

"What about this, then?" she said. "*The rat that gnaws at the cat's tail is asking for trouble.* That's interesting."

"That's one of Mum's sayings, not yours," scoffed Ping. "And anyway, it's not interesting because it's obvious. Only a mad rat would chew on a cat's tail."

"Exactly," said An. "That is why Mummy and I forbid you to get into a fight with a snow leopard because you will NEVER, EVER win!"

All of a sudden, the game was over and An was being serious.

"All right," said Ping. "Keep your fur on. You've made your point."

"Good," she said. "Because I am telling you now that if you are bonkers enough ever to take on a snow leopard, don't expect Mummy and me to scrape you off the forest floor."

Ping sighed. How could he ever expect

to inject a little excitement into his life when his mother and sister were always warning him off danger and telling him to be sensible?

"I've got a saying too," he said glumly. "*All food and no play makes Ping a dull panda!*"

"Food makes you healthy," An said smugly.

"Food makes me poo," said Ping, standing up and disappearing into the bushes. "If anyone wants me, I'm contemplating."

And so started Ping's day. It was just like every other day in the Wolagong Nature

Reserve: eating bamboo, disappearing into the bushes, suffering the mocking jibes of the golden monkeys and posing for the *clickety-clack* cameras of the visitors.

Ping's only real friend in the reserve was an electric-blue grandala bird called Hui, who had glossy feathers that gleamed like polished metal.

Just at that moment, Hui flew into the clearing and landed on the end of the bamboo stalk that Ping was slowly turning round in his mouth like a stick of seaside rock.

"Hui!" Ping cried. "How lovely to see you!"

Ping always liked talking to Hui. It was

Ping's belief that the brightly coloured grandala bird had a colourful life to match, whereas he, Ping, being only black and white, was condemned to a life without colour.

"Exciting news!" tweeted the grandala bird.

Ping pricked up his ears at the mention of excitement.

"I have just overheard the fat ranger talking about a panda exchange programme."

Wolagong Nature Reserve was looked after by a team of friendly rangers. The fat ranger was the one in charge, not because he was fat, but because he had more buttons on his jacket than any of the others.

"Oh," said Ping, who had never heard of a panda exchange programme before. "Is that exciting?"

"Well, I think it is," said Hui. "I overheard the rangers discussing it last night. Admittedly, I was a little distance away, but from what I could make out, they are planning to send one lucky panda from Wolagong Nature Reserve to London Zoo in England."

"On holiday?" Ping said. "I love holidays!"

"I suppose it is a sort of holiday," replied Hui. "It will certainly be different. London's not like Wolagong at all."

"That's my kind of town," declared Ping. "How do I get there?"

"That's simple," Hui replied. "We just have to make sure that the rangers choose you!"

Ping's heart sank. Now that he thought about it, he was sure they'd choose Gao. Gao posed for more photographs than any other panda in the nature reserve. Like Ping, he was still a cub, but he had the cute factor. It didn't seem fair to Ping that one cub should be cuter than another. He wanted to be cute too. But it was Gao who had the long eyelashes, fat cheeks and a way of looking up at the camera with his big black-and-white eyes that made grown-up visitors turn to jelly and lose their grasp of the English language.

"Oh, Wilma, hurnney, doncha jurst lurrrve that cutesy ikkle-wikkle cubby-wubby!" they cried. It made Ping sick.

But he refused to be downhearted.

"So let's assume it's between me and Gao," he said. "How do I give myself the edge over the pretty poser? How do I convince the rangers to pick me?"

"There's more to life than being pretty,"

said Hui. "Once, when I was flying past a school assembly in New Orleans, I heard the most beautiful sound drifting out of a window. It was a little girl playing the violin. That was when I learned that being talented was far more important."

"So you think I should learn to play a musical instrument?"

"Possibly," said the bird.

"Have you ever heard of an instrument called a piano?" asked the cub. "Do you think we could make one of those?"

"Pianos are rather large," said Hui practically. "If you're going to learn an instrument, it'll have to be one that we can make out of bamboo."

They sat in silence for the next ten minutes while they tried to think of one, but their combined minds drew a blank.

"How are you at dancing?" asked Hui. "I think we should forget music and explore the possibility that dancing might give you the edge."

"Dancing's a bit energetic for pandas," admitted Ping. "Unless I could dance sitting down."

Hui shook his head.

"I could recite some poetry."

"Do you know any?"

"Not really, but I could write some." Ping stood up and placed his paw across his chest in a strikingly theatrical pose.

"There's nothing I like more

Than a stick of old bamboo.

It gets the juices flowing

More than chewing on a shoe."

He looked to Hui for approval.

"What else can you do?" asked the wise bird.

They spent the next hour trying to identify those talents Ping possessed that might capture the imagination of the people who ran London Zoo. Would they choose a panda who could scratch his own back, or fold bamboo leaves into interesting shapes, or one that could wash his own toes by walking through a river? Maybe they would favour a whistling panda, or a cloud-counting panda, or a clever panda that knew sixty-three words for bamboo.

Eventually, Ping and Hui had to give in and admit that they did not know the first thing about London Zoo or what would appeal to the people in charge.

"They'll go for the pretty one, won't they," said Ping with a sigh of resignation. "We might as well give up now. They'll choose Gao, I know they will."

Suddenly, Hui jumped into the air and flapped his wings in a flurry of excitement.

"I've got it!" he cried. "A letter! A letter!"

"Which one?" asked Ping. "I know lots of them. A? B? M? T? U? V?"

47

"No. *You* write them a letter."

"Me? Write a letter? To whom?"

"The pandas who live at London Zoo. You write to them and ask them what life is like there. And when they write back and tell you, you'll know what it is you have to do to become the perfect panda for the exchange."

It was a glorious plan and one that Ping could not keep to himself for a moment longer. He ran to his mother, Mao Mao, and blurted it out. He even begged her to help him compose the letter, but to his surprise she refused.

"*Help*," she explained, "*is the thief of self-knowledge*."

Ping scratched his head.

"I don't know what you're talking about," he said.

"*A dragonfly tastes sweeter to a frog when snaffled by its own tongue.*"

"Why can't you ever speak normally?" he squeaked. "Will you help me write the letter or not?"

"*It is better to travel alone, Ping, for only then will you know when you have arrived.*"

Ping gave up.

"So you won't help me?" he said.

"No," she said, smiling. "*Sometimes it is kinder to be cruel, Ping. It's best you help yourself.*"

CHAPTER THREE

For three days Ping struggled to write his letter. His task was made all the more difficult by his sister hanging around behind him, trying to read what he was writing. It was very off-putting to hear her constantly chewing bamboo in his ear.

"Go away!" he shouted at her. "I can't hear myself think."

"I can stand here if I want to," An said. "It's a free world and I'm a protected species, so there's not much you can do about it, I'm afraid."

Ping blocked out the sound of his sister's voice by pressing his paws against his ears, but that made writing impossible. He needed his paws to hold the pen. So he tried holding the pen between his ear and his paw and leaning forward, but that didn't work because not only could he not read what he had written, but he ended up with ink splattered all over his cheek.

"You are the most annoying sister a brother

could ever have!" he exploded. "In fact, that's what I'm going to call you from now on. An-noying."

"Don't you dare," she warned him. But telling Ping not to do something was like waving a red rag in front of a bull.

"*An-noying,*" he sang. Then he kept on going until she burst into tears and ran away to tell Mummy. "*An-noying, An-noying, An-noying, An-noying, An-noying, An-noying, An-noying, An-noying...*"

Ping only stopped when his mother stamped her foot in front of him.

"What is going on?" she growled. "I was just sitting down to a lovely stick of bamboo when the peace and quiet was shattered by your sister's sobbing."

Ping explained how she had stopped him from writing his letter and for once, to his surprise, his mother took his side.

"Writing is the cornerstone of civilisation, An. *It is not for nothing that there is a duke inside every e-duke-ated panda!*" she said mysteriously. "Now come along. Let's go and suck on some bamboo and leave Ping to practise his writing."

Ping found it difficult to know where to start and the letter was scrunched up and thrown away a hundred times while he searched for the perfect opening.

~~Dear Sir~~

~~Dear Madam~~

~~Dear Panda~~

~~Dear Panda in London Zoo~~

~~Dear London Zoo Panda~~

~~Dear London Zoo~~

~~Hello, London~~

~~Hello~~

~~Wotcha~~

Greetings from the Wolagong Nature Reserve

Now *that* had dignity. And once he had made a start, the words flowed.

Greetings from the Wolagong
Nature Reserve

My name is Ping and I am the most handsome giant panda in all of China. In fact, people often remark on how much more handsome I am than Gao. So whatever you do, don't choose him. Remember the name Ping. I am just under a year old, have a glossy black-and-white coat and love to sit around chewing bamboo all day. I also have a good sense of humour and my hobbies include eating bamboo, having a poo forty-seven times a day and chatting to my best friend, Hui, about life, the universe and everything. My ambitions include flying to the moon and digging a hole through the earth to reach London. I've heard that London is a big city where the pavements are lined with bamboo and there are gold-plated toilets on every street corner. Is this true? And what is it like living in London Zoo? Here in Wolagong, the visitors just want to look at us being ourselves, but I imagine in a zoo they expect something a bit more exciting for their money... like pandas doing magic tricks, for example, or plate spinning. I can do both of these.

I am hoping to visit London Zoo soon,

So would appreciate any information
you can send me. I shall await your
reply with Chinese ants in my pants.
   Love Ping

Ping was true to his word. He gave the
letter to Hui to post via Bird Mail, then
sat around in the clearing with Chinese
ants in his pants. For the next three days,
he was a bundle of nerves, imagining his
letter flying over mountains, rivers, seas
and forests to reach the pandas in London
Zoo. He imagined them opening it and
gasping in excitement at their first contact
with a real panda from China. And he
imagined their reply to him gripped in

the talons of an eagle, taking off over the penguin pool and skimming through the clouds on its way back. But no matter how hard he imagined his reply arriving in the Wolagong Nature Reserve, it did not come.

His mother told him to be patient.

"Bamboo does not grow in a day," she said gravely.

Ping was aware of that, but what did the growth of bamboo have to do with Ping going to London Zoo; and while he was moaning, why did his mother always have to be so gloomy about everything? If she couldn't be more supportive about his adventure, he would share his plans with his twin sister instead.

"When this letter comes back, I'm going to London!" he boasted to An. "Where I'll be so famous that visitors will want to take my photograph all the time."

"In your dreams," she mocked. "London Zoo's not going to ask for *you* when they could have *me*, are they?"

"You!" exclaimed Ping, stunned by the ludicrous notion that his boring sister might seriously challenge him for first place on the London list. "Why would anyone in their right mind take a panda called An-*noying*?"

"Because," she said indignantly, "I am more beautiful than you; I am a better climber than you; I don't smell like stagnant water; and my name is An!"

"I don't smell like stagnant water," protested Ping.

"No. You smell like running water," she sniggered, "running through a poo-pit full of dead monkey brains and six hundred bad eggs wriggling with maggots."

"He who smelt it, dealt it," he said childishly. "And for the record, I'm a much better climber than you."

"OK," she said. "I accept your challenge!"

Then without waiting to say, 'Ready, steady, go!' An barged Ping out of the way with her stomach and ran towards the

nearest tree,
shouting, "Loser!"
over her shoulder.

Picking himself up, Ping
raced after her and started
climbing. He caught up near
the top of the tree, clambered
over her back and stretched out
to reach the highest branch. There
wasn't a claw's width in it – it was
a dead heat.

While they were sitting at the top
of the tree, An took a moment to
be serious.

"It's probably for the best," she said, "that the London pandas haven't written back."

"For you, maybe," said Ping, "but not for me."

"Yes, for me... I don't want you to leave," she said. "You're my twin brother. You're a part of me and if you go away, I'll miss you."

"It's only for an adventure," Ping said, giving his sister a hug. "I'll come back."

Nonetheless, it looked like An was going to get her wish. After three weeks of fruitless sky-watching, Ping finally gave up waiting. He sent his sister away, rejected all her attempts to play with him and curled up in a shady corner of the clearing.

"What's the matter?" asked his mother.

"I'm never going to leave this place," he sighed. "Hui said he'd be back with my answer in a couple of days. It's been weeks. Now I'm never going to find out what they're like in London. And if I don't know that, how am I ever going to impress the rangers?"

"*A bird only learns to fly when it stops trying to fly*," his mother said calmly.

"How can that be?" said Ping. "Surely if a bird stops trying to fly, it crashes to the ground!"

"I mean you should relax," she told him.

And sure enough, after five minutes of lying on his back, Ping had a brilliant idea. Flying! That was it. Of course. He could impress the rangers without the letter from London. A flying panda was guaranteed to stand out in a crowd. Who had ever seen a bear-bird before? He would be a star and London would beg him to visit. And if by some unfortunate misunderstanding he was still not picked for the panda exchange programme he could always fly himself to London.

I mean, how hard can it be to fly? he reasoned. Hui's been doing it since he was a little chick and he's tiny, whereas I am huge and my arms are massively strong. Once I get them flapping, I should be able to fly for miles…

So that was the plan.

All he needed to do now was find a way to get airborne. Launching his heavy body into the air was going to be the difficult part. Luckily, though, Ping was a panda who always looked on the bright side and believed that no problem was too hard to solve with some clever thinking.

"A catapult!" he shouted suddenly. "A giant panda catapult!"

It had been Hui who'd told Ping what a catapult was. Hui had seen a boy using one once to knock cans off a log. Ping's idea, therefore, was to build a large Y-shaped wooden frame out of bamboo and tie a creeper across the gap, which would stretch when he leant against it and then catapult him into the air when he took both feet off the ground at the same time.

And this was not the end of his brainwave because if he positioned his catapult on the edge of a very tall cliff, he would have further to fall before he hit the ground – and that would give him more time to master the technique of arm-flapping. The plan was nothing short of brilliant.

So he built his catapult on the ridge known as Do Not Feed The Bears Ridge because it had a Do Not Feed The Bears sign embedded in the grass on the summit. It took him almost a whole morning, and when he had finished, who should come nosing around but An.

"What are you doing?" she asked.

"Learning to fly," replied Ping, casually leaning back against the stretchy creeper.

An's black-and-white face turned white as she peered over the edge of the cliff.

"That's a long way down," she squeaked. "Isn't it a bit dangerous?"

"Of course it's dangerous," Ping told her. "If it wasn't dangerous I wouldn't get myself noticed, would I?"

"Then don't do it," begged An. "You'll

end up lying face down in the ravine, squashed as flat as a panda-pancake."

"No can do," he said, leaning back as far as he dared. "My mind's made up."

Then he lifted one foot off the ground and was just about to lift the other, when

there was an urgent cry from the sky.

"Ping!"

The panda cub looked up and could not contain his excitement.

"Hui!" he yelled. "At last! You're back!"

"Don't lift your other foot!" shouted the exhausted grandala bird.

"But I'm just about to make history," Ping replied. "Stick around and you'll see a giant panda fly!"

"Well, you might like to wait a second," urged Hui. "I've got a letter for you, Ping, all the way from London."

CHAPTER FOUR

Dear Ping

Greetings from London Zoo!

Hui flapped his wings like a hummingbird so that he could hover above Ping's head and read the letter over his friend's shoulder, while An jumped up and down behind her brother's back trying to get a proper view.

"Oh, please let me look!" she cried.

"No," he replied. "I know you. You'll only tell me not to go."

"You don't know what the letter says yet," she insisted. "And why would I tell you not to go?"

"Because you're not like me," said Ping. "You and Mum love it here in Wolagong, living life in the slow lane, sucking on bamboo and staring at the visitors. But I am an adventurer and this letter could be the beginning of my brilliant new life in London!"

He was so excited that he started to hiccup. "Now look what you've done," he said, standing on his head to make the hiccups go away. "Sit down over there and I'll let you see it when I've finished."

An moved away, picked up a stick of half-chewed bamboo and shoved it into her mouth, while Ping waited for the hiccups to ease off. Then he rolled himself the right way up again and smoothed out the piece of paper with a trembling paw.

Dear Ping

Greetings from London Zoo!

It's lucky your letter came to me because you and I are so alike. You are the most handsome panda in China, and I am the best-looking one in London. As a result I am the star attraction at London Zoo. The meerkats think it's them, but it's me, really. You only have to look at the long queues outside my enclosure to know that I am telling the truth. And that is without appearing in a stupid advert on TV, so I must be well popular.

I cannot recommend life in a zoo highly enough. It is like living in a posh hotel. Someone makes my bed every morning, room service is available day and night, and it doesn't matter where I go to the loo because there's always someone poised behind me with a mop and bucket. So what do I do all day? Well, apart from the usual panda stuff – eating, pooing and posing for cameras – I like throwing tea parties. I've got two close bear friends who regularly pop in for tea... Winnie the Pooh and Paddington Bear, who rather rudely brings his own marmalade sandwiches. Can you believe it? He doesn't like the taste of bamboo! I don't like the taste of cheese scones, but if that's what's on offer when I visit Buckingham Palace to take tea with The Queen, I eat them.

Did I mention that The Queen and I are very good friends? That's Queen Elizabeth the Second... or Liz, as I prefer to call her. She

often asks me over to walk her corgis while she's away opening a hospital or a school; and last week she asked me to design some blinds for her bathroom. I've chosen bamboo blinds because if she gets hungry in the middle of the night, she can eat them. When you come over, I'll introduce you, but you'll have to learn how to bow first. She is very particular about bowing.

That's it for now. Must go as I have a very busy day ahead. After I have eaten a stick of bamboo really slowly, I am planning to stare at some visitors. Can't wait to show you around!

Love Jack

PS Bring *an* umbrella. It never stops raining over here. In fact, it's raining cats and dogs right *now*!

PPS And bring *an* extra jumper because it is always cold!

Ping read the letter not once, not twice, but *three* times, and then finally out loud so that An could share in his excitement. Jack was clearly a very important panda – queens did not consort with any old riff-raff. Ping was going to London!

"'*Bring an umbrella!*'" he quoted to his twin sister. "Jack didn't say, '*If you come, bring an umbrella,*' but, '*Bring an umbrella.*'

It's a done deal. I'm going to London Zoo!"

"But it's not a done deal," An pointed out; "Not until the fat ranger sings."

Ping knew that An was right. That was another annoying thing about her – she *was* always right. To stand a chance of going to England, he would have to convince the fat ranger that he, Ping, was the perfect candidate.

So he devoted the rest of the day to making himself look as English as possible... by knitting himself a jumper out of moss and picking out a sturdy helmet from a family of tortoises, to fend off the cats and dogs when they started raining.

Then he took himself off into the forest

to practise his bowing. If the fat ranger could only see what a model English gentleman Ping was, then hopefully he, and not Gao, would be chosen to fly to London.

Unfortunately, Ping did not know what a bow was. He practised hard for several hours doing what he *thought* was a bow, but when he came to perform it the next morning in front of the fat ranger and a truckload of camera-snappy visitors, they just looked on dumbstruck – as in front of them danced a mossy-jumpered, tortoise-hatted panda, waving its arms and legs, and shaking its head, before turning round and waggling its bottom in the air in a manner so rude that frankly it would have shocked the Queen to the tip of her tiara. The fat ranger was convinced that Ping had some sort of fever and sent him to the vet's to rest.

His mother shook her head and said that she was not surprised.

"You've only got yourself to blame," she shouted after him as he was driven off. "Pandas are not designed to dance, Ping. *Pandas are to dance what elephants are to rollerskating.*"

🐾

Ever since he could remember, Ping did not like going to the vet's. There was always something unpleasant involved. If the vet wasn't sticking a big glass thermometer up Ping's bottom, or pressing down on Ping's tongue with a lollipop stick, he was making him take horrible-tasting medicine.

But today Ping did not like being at the vet's because it reminded him that he was useless at being English. And if he couldn't be English, the rangers wouldn't pick him to go to London. The dream would be over and Ping would just have to content himself with the humdrum life he already had – forty more years of bamboo, poos and touristy smiles. *There must be another way*, he thought as he drifted off to sleep.

CHAPTER FIVE

Ping's mother always said, *"Things look better after a good night's sleep."* But when Ping woke up the following morning, the only change he noticed was that his stomach had emptied and his bladder had filled. Neither of which made the world look particularly better.

As he was sitting in the forest sucking on a soggy stick of bamboo, Hui flew down from the uppermost branch of a katsura tree and landed on Ping's shoulder.

"Hello, Hui," Ping said. "I'm not going to London."

"Good," laughed Hui brightly.

"I'll never be an English gentleman."

"Even better!"

Ping regarded the bird suspiciously.

"*Even better*? How can you possibly say that? You were the one who encouraged me to go to London Zoo in the first place!"

"Because London's old news," replied Hui. "I overheard the fat ranger talking at breakfast-time this morning, and apparently this panda exchange programme is happening in Australia too."

"Ooh! Ooh! Ooh!" Ping was excited now. "I've heard of Australia! Remind me where it is again."

"Well, if you imagine the earth to be a round, juicy lychee," Hui explained, "China would be right in the middle, while England would be at the top and Australia underneath at the bottom."

"Oh, yes, I like the sound of underneath," smiled Ping.

"Why?" asked Hui.

"Because that means that everything in Australia must be upside down."

"How do you work that out?"

"When a fruit fly lands on the bottom of a lychee, it hangs upside down, doesn't it?" said Ping. "So it stands to reason that people and animals would hang upside down in Australia too."

"Forgive me, but I fail to see why that would be a good thing," said Hui.

"It's not a question of good or bad. It's *different*," said the panda cub.

So Ping wrote a second letter and addressed it to the pandas in Adelaide Zoo. He requested any information they could give him on the Australian way of life so that he could impress the Wolagong rangers with his knowledge of that country and prove himself the most suitable candidate for the exchange programme.

Hui duly delivered the letter – and a week later, Ping received a letter in reply.

Dear Ping

G'day from Adelaide, where it's hotter than a koala chomping on chilli con carne! There are only two giant pandas down here in the southern hemisphere, which makes us pretty special. There's me, Adelaide (yup, named after the zoo!), and my best friend, Henry. Obviously, he's not my only friend. I mean, this is Australia, the friendliest country on earth, where people cuddle sharks and kiss crocodiles. If you've never seen a crocodile, Ping, imagine a long baguette with teeth. That's French bread to you and me. Terrifying. Anyway, you wanted to know what we do in this Aussie zoo. Well – a lot of sport, mate. After dark, when the visitors have gone home for their tucker, we come out of our pens and enclosures and play a few games. Now, clearly, some of the animals have got an advantage. The swordfish is particularly good at fencing, although he can't stay out

88

of the water for more than thirty seconds without turning blue; the gorillas are great at Aussie Rules football; and the kangaroos are ace at cricket cos they can catch the ball in their pouches. Well, I say a ball, but we use a rolled-up armadillo. They're two a penny down here, so if one gets dented or scuffed up, we can just change him. No problem.

I hear what you're asking, Ping. What are we giant pandas good at? I'll tell you what we're NOT good at, mate, and that's bungee jumping! I don't mind admitting that when

I was hurtling to the ground at two hundred miles an hour, I was petrified. I kept thinking that the python wrapped round my ankles was going to snap. Anyway, Henry and I are fantastic at surfing. It's because you don't have to move, you see. There's a lot of lying down on a board, paddling out to a big wave and then standing up. And I don't need to tell you that we pandas are great at lying down and standing up. So what do you say, Ping? Are you up for catching a big white one and riding the wave?! Cowabunga, dude!

Adelaide

Well, if that was what Aussie pandas did, Ping would have to learn how to do it too.

"But Sichuan Province is miles from any sea," said Hui, who foresaw big trouble if Ping went hunting the surf in Wolagong.

"How else am I going to show the rangers that I'm perfect for the exchange programme?" protested Ping. "Teach me how to surf, dude."

"But it's stupidly dangerous, and you don't like water."

Ping tried to sound cool.

"*Fear is only fun, but spelt differently*," he said casually.

"Now you sound ridiculous – just like your mother," observed Hui. "Besides, where are you going to find a three-metre wave to surf on in the Wolagong Nature Reserve?"

The panda cub's eyes twinkled with mischief.

"Have you never heard of the River Trickle?" he asked.

"Of course I have," said the grandala bird. "It slides slowly down the face of Mount Tranquil like a teardrop. But it's called the Trickle for a reason, Ping. It's a trickle! You couldn't surf a leaf on that."

"Maybe not as it is," said Ping ominously, "but there's a saying. *From teeny tiny trickles do massive great roaring rivers flow.*"

"Oh, dear," muttered Hui nervously. "Why do I think we're all going to get wet?"

CHAPTER SIX

Needless to say, Ping had made up that saying about '*great roaring rivers*', but it sounded like the sort of thing a clever person would say, and besides, it perfectly described his cunning plan.

So, he decided that the first thing to

do was to build himself a surfboard out of bamboo poles – and then swell the River Trickle by adding lots of water.

For the next few days, Ping left the family enclosure early in the morning and came back late at night, exhausted and covered in dirt. His sister, An, who liked unpicking a secret, was bursting to know what he was up to, and after three nights of mysterious brotherly silence, she finally snapped.

"I can't bear it any longer," she said to him on the third night. "What *are* you up to? You're gone all day and when you do come home you jump straight into bed without a bath."

"None of your business," he replied, resting his head on his paws and closing his eyes. "Let's just say I'm looking after my future."

"You're digging a tunnel to England, aren't you, so that you can crawl to London Zoo!"

"That is the most ridiculous thing I have ever heard," laughed Ping, keeping his answer irritatingly vague.

"So what *are* you doing?" she persisted, rolling over and prodding him in the ribs.

Ping stood up and slipped something out from underneath his mattress of rhododendron leaves. It was one and a half metres long and looked like a large bamboo tea tray.

"You're planning to serve tea?" she asked, confused.

"That's for me to know and you to find out," he said secretively.

"You're planning to serve English tea to the rangers so that they will think you're an English gentleman and send you to London Zoo?"

Ping raised his eyebrows haughtily.

"London is so yesterday," he scoffed.

"Meaning what?" she squeaked in frustration. "If you don't tell me what you're doing, I'll tell Mummy you're up to no good and she'll *make* you confess."

"Tell me what?" Their mother's voice

pierced the darkness like the snap of a twig.

"Nothing!" shouted Ping, kicking his sister for being so loud.

"Ow!" she yelped. "You'll pay for that."

"Go to sleep," ordered Mao Mao. "It's late."

In the dark, Ping could hear An sniggering.

"Now you'll have to tell me," she said. "Because if you don't, I'll scream and that will get Mummy out of bed, and I will tell her you kicked me and she will be so furious that you will be grounded for a year!"

Ping knew when he was beaten. Besides,

if he drew his sister into the plan, maybe she could help.

"Right," he said. "Here's the deal. Tomorrow lunchtime, I want you to lure all the rangers and visitors to the wooden bridge that crosses the River Trickle. If you do, I promise to share my secret with you. But until then, you mustn't let on that something spectacular is going to happen."

"Is it really going to be spectacular?" whispered An excitedly.

"A sight so rare that it has only ever been seen in Australia," boasted Ping.

"Gosh!" his sister muttered in awe. "It sounds completely brilliant."

"It will be," said Ping. "Now, can I borrow a skirt?"

The next day, Ping had until lunchtime to carry out the second part of his plan – to make the River Trickle roar! He left the enclosure before sunrise and climbed the mountain to the source of the river.

As the sun's first rays sparkled across the water, Ping arrived in his chosen clearing, laid down his bamboo surfboard and pulled on his sister's skirt. It was her best party skirt, made from the finest grass, and it rustled when he wiggled his hips.

He had come out this early partly so that no other panda would see him wearing girls' clothes and partly to give his plan time to work. He was going to make it rain, and the rain was going to fill up the river – and a full river would provide the perfect conditions for surfing.

But first he had to perform a rain dance. Hui had once told him about people in faraway Papua New Guinea who wore ceremonial skirts, shoved bones through their noses and danced beneath the clouds to make the rain fall. They sang a special rain song, apparently, which Hui had not been able to remember, so Ping decided to make something else up instead.

Not having a bone, he shoved a short length of bamboo between his teeth, then,

hopping from paw to paw as if dancing on a seesaw, he gazed up at the sky, and in his politest voice, intoned the following ditty.

"Oh, weeping wet clouds
Up high in the sky,
Burst into tears and
Spit in my eye.
If we are best mates,
Release your floodgates.
Not spitters and spatters
It's monsoons what matters."

The last line was rather poor, but Ping was starting to feel sick from jiggling up and down, and to be honest, he couldn't think of anything better. He stopped to catch his breath and held out a paw to see if it was raining.

It wasn't.

Then suddenly he remembered what Jack had said about it raining cats and dogs in England. Maybe *that* was what he was doing wrong.

"Here, pussy-pussy!" he shouted up at the clouds. "Come to Pingy!" And then in a slightly crosser voice – because that is what dogs respond to – he added, "Bad boy! Naughty boy! Come down out of that cloud NOW and fall into the river!"

Still nothing.

Ping was starting to become desperate. He improvised a dance by doing several forward somersaults and then running round in a figure of eight, while making the sort of noises that he imagined cats and dogs would understand.

"*Woof!*" he
barked. "*Woof,
woof, woof,
woof! Miaow,
miaow, woof,
miaow.*"

But still nothing.

Wherever the cats and dogs might be lurking, it certainly wasn't up in the clouds.

The only animals he *did* attract were the golden monkeys, who had rushed through the forest to see what all the noise was about, and finding Ping dancing around in his sister's skirt, barking like a mad dog, they fell out of the trees with laughter.

"Haven't you got anything better to do?" shouted Ping, his face reddening as the laughter grew louder.

"What could be better than this?" screeched Choo. "Watching you dance is much funnier than stealing cameras from tourists, taking pictures of our bottoms, then putting the cameras back in their pockets… And THAT is funny!"

Ping slunk away into the undergrowth to reassess his plan. It was now nine o'clock and he had wasted two hours trying to make it rain. If the surf was to be up by lunchtime, he needed to move fast. It was time for Plan B.

Chinese beavers!

Now Ping knew that Chinese beavers would do anything for a cup of Chinese tea, so he offered them a steaming pot of the stuff if they'd build a dam across the River Trickle, let the water build up behind it, and then break the dam so that the water would gush down the mountainside in a tidal wave.

What Ping did not realise, however, was that along with the tea drinking, went the tea drinking *ceremony*, and the beavers were sticklers for detail. The beaver leader, a buck-toothed fellow called Fang, explained what was going to happen.

First, everyone had to sit in a circle and look at the tea leaves in the bottom of the teapot for half an hour before Ping was allowed to pour the boiling water over them. Then the tea had to infuse for the correct amount of time.

"An hour!" gasped Ping.

"For maximum flavour," nodded Fang.

And finally there was the sniffing, which went on forever while the teapot was passed round and the heavenly tea-soaked steam was sniffed through the snout.

Ping was getting anxious. At one o'clock, if An had done her job, a crowd would be gathering on the wooden bridge, expecting to see something spectacular. And if Ping was to be chosen to go to Australia, instead of pretty-boy Gao, he needed to be cresting a wave on his surfboard and whooshing past at that precise moment.

It was now twelve o'clock, the tea had still not been drunk, and Ping had run out of time.

"Forget it!" he shouted, jumping to his feet in a panda panic. "It'll have to be Plan C."

Plan C was the third-best plan because Ping thought it stood the least chance of succeeding. Somehow, he had to convince the golden monkeys to help him – despite the fact that the golden monkeys were famous for never helping anyone and always doing the opposite of what they were asked to do...

Ping would have to think creatively.

Stopping briefly by a Chinese ants' nest, Ping plunged his arm down the hole at the top and grabbed some ants. Then, ignoring the sharp pinpricks on the ends of his paws where the ants had started to bite him, he ran as fast as he could to the clearing where the monkeys had made fun of him earlier. They were still there, lounging on top of a big rock by the side of the river, asleep in the sunshine. Ping crept between the snoring bodies and sprinkled the ants round the base of the rock. Then he stepped back and coughed loudly.

The monkeys woke with a start, their heads still foggy with sleep, and before they could properly come to their senses, Ping made an announcement.

"I thought you might like to know," he said, with the air of someone who couldn't care less, "that I think you're sleeping on top of a nest of Chinese ants."

That woke the monkeys up! They leapt off the rock and stuck their greedy faces to the ground, where the first thing they saw, of course, was a swarm of Chinese ants!

Ping knew enough about golden monkeys to understand that they would move heaven and earth to get at a nest of these deliciously crunchy insects. Only on this occasion, moving heaven and earth would not be necessary because all they had to move was a rock.

So while the monkeys heaved and strained to move the rock off the non-existent nest, Ping added the final cunning twist to his plan by casually reminding them that the rangers had expressly

forbidden anyone to push rocks into the Trickle in case they should block the river.

Minutes later, of course, there was a large rock lying in the middle of the river, blocking the flow and causing the water to build up fast behind it. Ping had achieved the first stage of his goal with a magnificent lie – and still had five minutes to spare.

The only problem now was that with the rock rolled away, the monkeys could see there was no ants' nest underneath.

"Maybe they're hiding," suggested Ping.

"How stupid do you think we are?" screeched Gang, the fiercest of the monkeys. "Millions of ants can't just run away and hide!"

"Well, maybe they've packed their bags and gone away on holiday."

"You lied to us," growled Choo. "You made up the story about the ants' nest to trick us into moving that rock."

"OK, I admit it; I'm sorry," said the panda cub. "But whatever you do," he added slyly, "when I stand on my surfboard on top of it in approximately five minutes' time, you must NOT push the rock away, in case the water explodes down the mountain in a gigantic gush and takes me with it."

Luckily, the golden monkeys knew nothing about the mechanics of surfing – and even less about the brilliantly devious mind of a certain panda cub called Ping!

And so it was that five minutes later, as Ping's sister lured a crowd of rangers and tourists on to the wooden bridge by sitting on the other side and looking especially cute, the spectators heard a loud explosion on the mountain above them. It sounded like a giant paddling pool bursting, and was followed by a menacing rumble that grew louder and louder until suddenly, around the trees, a wall of white water swirled into view, with a screaming panda cub on a bamboo board balancing on top – although he *wasn't* balancing. He was upside down, and left and right, and round and round, and flailing this way and that like a tumbling black-and-white sock in a washing machine. Clinging on to his surfboard for dear life, Ping swept past the astonished crowd, hit a submerged tree trunk and took off.

"Heeeeeeeeelp!" he wailed as he flew past a wide-eyed Hui with all the grace of a fat penguin. "Tell my mother I love her!" And then, like the setting sun, he disappeared behind a bamboo hedge and hit the ground with a *squelch*.

When Ping woke up, he was back at the vet's with a bandage wrapped round his head.

"What happened?" he asked weakly of the fuzzy faces that floated in and out of focus round his bed.

"You've had a bit of an accident," said a voice that sounded like his mother's.

"Is that why I feel like I've just swallowed a water buffalo?" Ping croaked. "Full of water."

"It's your own fault," the voice continued. "You know what they say – *A dry panda is a cuddly panda, but a wet panda is a fish*." It was definitely his mother.

"He's leaking like a fish," said his sister. "There's water all over the floor."

"You are a giant panda, Ping, not James Bond. Your life is not meant to be exciting. If you're not careful, you'll end up in here permanently," said Mao Mao.

"But did I do it?" he asked. "Did I surf the big one?"

"No," said An flatly. "You fell down a large mountain on a tea tray. There was no skill involved at all."

"Weren't the rangers impressed?"

"The fat ranger was impressed by your surfboard when it dented his head," sniggered An.

"So I won't be going to Australia then?"

"Was *that* what your secret was about?" she said disappointedly. "Trying to get yourself chosen by the rangers to go abroad again?"

Ping nodded his sore head.

"It was probably best I didn't get

chosen," he muttered. "I don't think I'm cut out for surfing."

"Or flying," added Hui, who had popped in through the open window to visit his friend. "I would have been here sooner, but I got held up at the office. The rangers wanted everyone to hang around while they praised Gao for his bravery."

"Bravery?" said Ping. "Please tell me it wasn't Gao who came to my rescue when I wiped out on the big wave?"

"No. Gao was far too busy elsewhere to save you," said Hui. "He was rescuing the rangers' hats after they'd been swept away by the water."

Ping groaned.

"I should have known that Gao would end up being the hero," he said gloomily. "I'm the one who takes the risks and he's the one they send to Australia."

"Be not jealous of another man's talent," his mother said, *"lest that jealousy devours your own talent instead."*

"Ping doesn't have a talent," smirked An. "Unless you count having a talent for being talentless!"

"I'm not jealous of Gao," Ping said indignantly, "but it's not fair if the only reason he gets to travel the world is because he's cute."

At that moment, the vet entered the room. He was carrying a clipboard and writing something down on a piece of paper.

"Right, Ping," he said, "you can go home now. But do try to take a little more care in future."

Ping leapt out of bed like an overeager jack-in-a-box.

"What excellent timing," declared Hui. "Let's get out of here, Ping. I've got something rather interesting to tell you."

CHAPTER SEVEN

The first thing Ping vowed to do when he left the vet's was never to return, but so exciting was Hui's news that this vow was instantly forgotten.

"While I was in the hut watching Gao being given an extra ration of bamboo for saving the rangers' hats—"

"I bet they rewarded him with a ticket to Australia as well," Ping grumbled.

"That's what I'm trying to tell you!" squawked the grandala bird. "I saw a chart on the fat ranger's noticeboard. It said 'Panda Exchange Programme' and underneath there was a list of countries from all round the world – England, Australia, Austria, Scotland, Spain and Thailand. And each country had a tick next to it."

"Ugh!" shuddered Ping. "I hate ticks. They leave their heads in your skin when you try to pull them out."

"Not bloodsucking ticks!" exclaimed

Hui. "Ticks. Marks of approval. Symbols of Yes-ness."

"What about names?" asked Ping, sounding a bit more interested. "Was the name 'Ping' on the board next to one of the countries?"

"No," said the bird. "Just ticks."

Ping looked disappointed and not a little sad. The light went out in his big black eyes again as the hope of an adventure went up in smoke.

"It's not a bad thing," said Hui encouragingly. "It means that a panda exchange *is* going to take place with that country, but they haven't decided which panda to send yet."

"So… I'm still in with a chance?" Ping asked hopefully, raising his head.

"I don't see why not," said Hui.

"What were the names of those other countries again?"

"Austria, Scotland, Spain and Thailand," came Hui's reply. "Why?"

"Because I've got four very important letters to write!" Ping shrieked. And despite being sore from his visit to the vet's, he allowed himself a jink, a jig, two jaunty jumps and a belly-wobbling hip-wiggle. A life of travel and excitement was still there for the taking!

But this time Ping had to get a move on. With four letters to write, he didn't have time for small talk. He had to get to the point and leave the giant pandas who were reading his words in no doubt that he, Ping, was the one and only panda in the world that they simply HAD to meet.

In order to keep things brief, Ping decided to send postcards instead of letters, and Hui happily agreed because postcards were lighter and less tiring to deliver. Then they set about their task.

After Hui had told Ping everything he knew about Austria, Scotland, Spain and Thailand, Ping wrote the cards in double-quick time and Hui's Bird Mail scattered them to the four corners of the earth.

But days passed and no replies came.

"The letters won't arrive any quicker if you worry, Ping," said his mother for the millionth time, as she caught Ping gazing anxiously up at the clouds again.

"I'm not worrying," he replied tetchily.

"Yes, you are," his sister chipped in as she relaxed on the ground with her legs in the air, munching on a stick of bamboo. "There's a tremendous air of tension around you, Ping, that's putting me off my food."

"You don't look put off," Ping said. "You look positively put *on*! I've never seen anyone as laid back as you while they were eating."

"*Never hurry a curry*," his mother slipped

into the conversation.

"But it's not a curry, is it?" Ping pointed out. "She's eating a stick of bamboo."

"OK, then," his mother countered. "*Never rush through a stick of bamboo!*"

🐾

Then at last, nine days later, the first reply arrived. It was from a giant panda called Viveka who lived in Vienna, Austria. Ping learnt:

To be famous in Austria, you have to be either a skier or a baker. I am a fabulous baker and have won many international baking competitions with my signature cake

– the Viennese Victoria Dundee Lemony Spongy Fruity Nutty Jammy Cupcake. I shall post you a slice when I make my next one, although I suspect it won't reach you as, no doubt, the postman will eat it on the long flight between Austria and China. You can't trust a bird when there are crumbs around.

Skiing! Now that was a sport fit for pandas. It took Ping two days to chisel out his bamboo skis and a further three days to trudge to the snow-capped peak of Mount Tranquil with them tied to his back. All this did was delay his return to the vet's by five days. For at first light on the morning of the sixth day, he strapped the skis to his feet and with a cry of "*Hupzekneesundboompsadaisy!*" he launched himself off the peak.

It took him less than eight seconds to reach a cruising speed of a hundred kilometres an hour – and one second more to hit the tree.

Ping lay in the snow, waiting for the ambulance to turn up, and mentally struck Austria off the list.

After a sleepover at the vet's, Ping came out to discover that a second reply had arrived. He found it in his sister's mouth.

"What are you doing?" he cried as he tugged the message from between her teeth.

"I'm trying to eat it," she said. "I don't want you to get hurt again."

The postcard was from a giant panda called Hamish, who lived in Scotland. It told him:

YOU CAN DO ONE OF THREE THINGS TO GET YOURSELF NOTICED IN SCOTLAND.

1) PLAY THE BAGPIPES — BUT EVERYONE SEEMS TO DO THAT UP HERE NOW SO IT'S NOT VERY SPECIAL; 2) SCOTTISH DANCING — FORGET IT. THAT'S WHAT I DO AND I DON'T WANT YOU TREADING ON MY TOES. I RECENTLY PERFORMED A HIGHLAND FLING ON TV'S STRICTLY COME SCOTTISH DANCING AND RECEIVED AN IMPRESSIVE SCORE FROM THE JUDGES; 3) TOSSING THE CABER — TRUE SCOTTISH HEROES ARE MEN WHO CAN TOSS CABERS AND I WOULD RECOMMEND THAT YOU START TRAINING FOR THAT.

After Hui had explained that a caber was a tree trunk, and had employed a family of woodpeckers to chop down a tree and strip off the branches, Ping tried to lift it up. He wrapped his arms round the wood and strained... and heaved... and puffed... and finally dropped to the floor with cramp.

PUFF

PANT

?

His sister, who had come along to watch, let out a small laugh.

"You can't even lift it, let alone toss it," she said. "Say goodbye to Scotland, Ping. Stay here in Wolagong where you belong."

"I will not be defeated," her brother wheezed from the floor. "I need to build up my strength before I can tackle the whole tree. I need to start by tossing smaller things."

Being a twin, An understood what her brother meant before the words were even out of his mouth. She tried to run, but Ping was too quick.

"No!" she cried as he grabbed her by

the legs. "I don't want to be a caber."

"Don't be such a baby," he said. "It won't hurt."

But it did.

An was fine, but Ping pulled a muscle in his back and spent another night at the vet's.

🐾

Luckily, the third postcard arrived just as he was feeling better. It was a short one from Spain, in which a panda called Manuel recommended that Ping became a bullfighter to increase his chances of being sent to Madrid.

REAL BEARS FIGHT BULLS.

Obviously there were no bulls in
the Wolagong Nature Reserve, but
by persuading three monkeys
to sit on each other's
shoulders and charge
at him with
sharpened
bamboo
poles,
Ping
was

able to practise his bullfighting moves using a cape made from bamboo leaves.

Unfortunately, he had forgotten that the monkeys were still angry about his rolling-rock-river-ant-nest trick, and the moment he turned his back, they leapt down and kicked his bottom.

This time when Ping emerged from the vet's, he was walking rather gingerly and carrying a cushion to sit on.

"I know something that will put a smile on your face," squawked Hui, holding out the fourth reply. "I've got another postcard."

Despite his bruised bottom, Ping's enthusiasm for a life of adventure remained as strong as ever, and he read the text with a glint in his eye. It was from Thailand, from a panda called Nattapong.

HERE IN CHIANG MAI WE LEAD A SPIRITUAL LIFE, CONTEMPLATING NATURE AND LISTENING TO THE GOODNESS INSIDE OURSELVES. HOWEVER, TOO MUCH SITTING DOWN AND THINKING EVENTUALLY LEADS TO FAT BELLIES. WE THEREFORE FOLLOW A STRICT EXERCISE REGIME HERE AT THE ZOO THAT INVOLVES THREE HOURS OF THAI KICK-BOXING EVERY DAY. MODESTY FORBIDS ME FROM MENTIONING THAT I AM NOW BRILLIANT AT IT AND HAVE ACHIEVED THE STATUS OF GRAND MASTER. PERHAPS YOU SHOULD BRUSH UP YOUR BOXING SKILLS IF YOU WISH TO VISIT.

So Ping threw himself into kick-boxing training, with Hui as his coach. Every day for a week, he got up before dawn and as the sun rose, he shadow-boxed with shadows, wrestled with rocks, kicked down fields of bamboo and punched a punchbag made from a hollowed-out towel gourd.

And in that week he was injured only once, when the punchbag swung back, hit him in the face and gave him two black eyes.

Luckily, when his mother came to visit him at the vet's for the sixth time in as many weeks, she didn't notice the black eyes because a panda's eyes are black all the time.

It was Hui who broke the bad news while Ping lay stretched out on his hospital bed with a bag of ice on his forehead.

"I'm afraid the chart hasn't changed," he said. "Your name still isn't on it."

"So I'm not going anywhere?" Ping sighed, wondering what he had to do to get noticed. "After all my efforts to get away, I've ended up exactly where I started."

"There's nothing wrong with staying in one place," said his mother, who was sitting on the other side of the bed to Hui. "There's no place like home, Ping. Be happy with your lot, and remember – *The tiger who never stops chasing his tail eventually turns into butter.*"

Mao Mao's voice drifted off into a bank of sleepy clouds as Ping closed his eyes. Maybe his mother was right. Maybe it was time to stop dreaming of a life full of adventure and start learning to live with what he'd got. After all, it had to be better than spending his life at the vet's.

CHAPTER EIGHT

A week later, Ping was lying in a clearing far away from his usual patch, chewing on a bamboo leaf. He was on a stakeout – hiding behind a clump of tall grass and spying on his rival, Gao, while he went about his daily business.

It was both a surprise and a relief to see that Gao was still on the reserve and wasn't showing any signs of leaving soon. Ping had expected to find him packing his bags, ready for the big flight out of there, but that was clearly not the case.

This left Ping rather baffled. If neither he nor Gao were being sent abroad as part of the panda exchange, who was?

A squawk from above disturbed his thoughts. Ping looked up just as Hui flew down and parked his brightly coloured feathers beside him.

"You are hard to find, my friend," the grandala bird said.

"I don't want people to see me," Ping

replied. "To tell the truth, I feel rather
stupid, Hui. I tried to learn all those
impressive skills and I failed at each and
every one of them."

Ping was surprised to see Hui blush. For a brief moment his blue face seemed to turn red.

"Actually," Hui said sheepishly, "I think it's me who failed. I was in the fat ranger's hut last night and heard him explaining how the panda exchange programme is going to work… and I think I may have made a teeny tiny mistake."

"What do you mean, *mistake?*" Ping wasn't sure if he wanted to hear this.

"Those ticks on that chart on the noticeboard…"

"Yes?"

"Well, obviously, they still mean exactly what I said… I got that bit right.

Well done me... Those *are* the countries that the exchange will take place with. But that's as far as me being right went, I'm afraid. Instead of pandas from Wolagong going overseas, pandas from England, Australia, Austria, Scotland, Spain and Thailand are coming here!"

It took a moment for the news to sink in.

"You mean, all those pandas I wrote to are visiting *us*?" gasped Ping.

"All of them," squawked Hui excitedly. "Tomorrow, there's going to be a great big Panda Party here in Wolagong!"

"Tomorrow?"

Hui waited for Ping to share his excitement, but Ping just looked horrified, as if he'd been caught doing something really naughty.

"Tell me you're teasing," he whimpered. "Tell me this is all a bad dream."

"Why?" said Hui. "I thought you'd be pleased."

"But you don't know what I've done," quivered Ping.

"No, I don't," said Hui. "What? Spit it out, Ping, for goodness' sake!"

"Well, my letters…" he began falteringly. "I didn't believe people would think I was interesting… So I may have… What I'm trying to say, Hui, is that it's just possible that I may have exaggerated a *tiny little bit*."

"Exaggerated what?" screamed Hui.

"The story of ME!" shouted the panda cub. "What I do. What I am. What I've achieved!"

"But you haven't achieved anything," said the grandala bird. "And you don't *do* much either, except sleep a lot, eat bamboo and poo forty-seven times a day."

"That's why I did it," blurted out Ping, who was as close to tears as Hui had ever seen him. "That's why I lied."

"Stop," said the bird. "Take a deep breath. These things are never as bad as you imagine them to be. Tell me what you wrote and we'll decide if there's a problem."

So Ping told Hui what he'd written.

"Well, first I told London Jack that I could do magic tricks and plate spinning, and then I told Adelaide Adelaide that I could cook bamboo on a barbecue!"

"What's wrong with that?" said Hui.

"Nothing," said Ping. "But I should have stopped there because then I told Viveka in Austria that I had the fur for winter sports, which was why I'd been selected for the Chinese Winter Olympics team."

"OK," said Hui. "So she thinks you're a Winter Olympian. That's not so bad."

"It gets worse," whispered Ping. "When I wrote to Hamish in Scotland I told him that I was half Scottish, which was why I called myself Ping McPing and wore my sister's skirts!"

Hui raised an eyebrow in surprise.

"And I went on to tell him that I was a very famous classical bagpipe player, who played all the classic tunes by all the best classical bagpipe composers – Beethoven, Mozart and Justin Bieber… I wanted him to ask me over to Glasgow to play, you see."

The grandala bird rubbed his beak thoughtfully.

"Tricky," he said. "So now they think you're a plate-spinning, bamboo-cooking, classical bagpipe-playing Winter Olympian who wears a skirt."

"And the truth is, I don't know any classical music," squealed Ping.

"You surprise me," said the grandala bird. "Do you know any music for bagpipes?"

"No!" Ping cried, his voice beginning to wobble with nerves. "I don't even know what a bagpipe looks like!"

"What's next?" asked Hui, keen to press on before the panda cub became too upset to speak.

"Manuel in Spain," said Ping. "This one was really silly. I told him that there was a sport here in China that requires more courage than bullfighting."

"And which sport is that exactly?"

"Dragon-fighting!" blurted Ping. "I told

him I was really good at putting out a dragon's fiery breath."

"And did you tell him *how* you put out a dragon's fire?"

"Yes. I said I stole the fire extinguishers from the fat ranger's office. I'm in trouble, aren't I?" trembled the little panda.

"Not at all," said Hui, who by now was starting to look every bit as nervous as Ping. "As long as tomorrow, when these pandas visit us, you can pull off being a skirt-wearing, plate-spinning, bamboo-cooking, classical bagpipe-playing Winter Olympian, who also happens to be a part-time dragon-fighter, I think you'll be fine."

"Is that a joke?" asked the panda.

"Yes," replied the bird. "Is that all?"

"I wish it was," said Ping, his voice quaking with fear. "My last postcard was sent to Nattapong in Thailand and I think I got rather carried away. I told him that... um... my name was Ping."

"But that's true!"

"*Emperor* Ping."

Ping gulped nervously and waited for Hui's verdict.

"I think it would be fair to say," concluded Hui, after much consideration, "that you have stretched the truth further than the waistband of the fat ranger's trousers."

"I'm not really an Emperor," said Ping.

"No. I know," said Hui dryly.

Hui walked around the clearing to get things straight in his head. When he returned to Ping's side he was smiling.

"Well," he said, "one thing's for sure, Ping... that's some imagination you've got there, but I don't think there's any harm done. When the other pandas arrive you'll just have to tell them the truth."

"But they'll think I'm a liar," Ping cried.

"You are," said the straight-talking bird.

"And none of them will like me," wailed Ping.

"I still like you," said Hui, "and I know the truth."

"But you're different," Ping said. "I've

known you all my life."

"It will all be fine," the bird said, putting a comforting wing around Ping's shoulder. "Trust me."

But Ping was not so sure. That his lies should be exposed like this in the cold light of day… what a first-class nincompoop he had been. What on earth was he going to do? There was only one thing for it…

CHAPTER NINE

The next morning, Wolagong Nature Reserve was a hive of activity, but not because the giant pandas were arriving from all over the world for a party. It was because Ping was missing.

Mao Mao and An were sitting anxiously

outside the fat ranger's office, waiting for news. An leant her head against her mother's chest and sobbed hysterically, while Mao Mao gently stroked the fur on the top of her daughter's head.

"Do you think he's dead?" An wailed.

"No," said her mother. "The fat ranger knows what he's doing."

"But he can't look after himself, Mummy. He's too young. And he's a boy. We have to find him."

"They're doing everything they can," she said. "Hui is out there helping too."

"What if Ping's fallen off a cliff?"

"He won't have fallen off a cliff."

"Or jumped. That would be worse.

Maybe he was practising to be a bungee jumper and forgot to attach the bungee to a tree at the top! Oh, Mummy," she howled, "I'm so sad!"

Mao Mao gave her daughter a hug, and smiled at just how alike her two children were. *"Where there is panic, there is no room for imagination,"* she muttered to herself. *"But where there is no panic, imagination is king and rules uncontrolled until panic arrives."*

The truth was that Ping had run away… with a rucksack of bamboo strapped to his back, just in case he never found food again. He had crept out of bed before dawn and struck out into the darkness

 without a thought for where he was going. All he knew was that he had to get away. He could not stay and face the humiliation of being branded a fibber in front of his foreign friends and then being forced to tell the truth – that he was just an ordinary cub who slept a lot, ate bamboo and went for a poo forty-seven times a day. They'd be so disappointed in him. They might even hate him, despite what Hui said.

No, the most important thing was to

run away and stick his head in a hole so that he wouldn't be able to see his new friends and they wouldn't be able to see him.

So it came as something of a shock when Ping heard a familiar beating of wings and, looking up, saw Hui hovering above his head.

"Found you!" shouted the grandala bird. "The rangers are hunting for you."

"*Hunting?*" Ping gasped. "Have they got guns?"

"I just meant they're looking for you," said Hui.

"Why?" Ping felt trapped. "Have they found out that I've been telling lies? Have

I given Wolagong a bad name? They're not sending me away, are they?"

"I thought you wanted to go away," cried Hui.

"Yes, but not in disgrace. They might send me to prison!"

"For telling a fib?" laughed the bird. "Don't be silly!"

"Well, I'm not hanging around to find out," said the frightened panda cub.

And with that he turned to run off into the bush, only to find that his escape route was blocked by a khaki-coloured Jeep that screeched to a halt in front of him.

Instinctively, Ping backed away – until he saw the face of the man who jumped out of the driving seat. Ping knew him. It was the ranger they called Mr Ho.

"Whoa there, boy," Mr Ho said, stretching out his arms to calm Ping down. "No need to be scared. We've been looking all over the place for you."

Something in the top pocket of the man's jacket crackled and fizzed and made Ping jump. "Yes, I've found him," the ranger said quietly into his radio. "It's amazing how far he's travelled. This is one feisty cub. Don't worry, I'll turn him around and guide him back as gently as I can. Someone's going to have to come out and pick up the Jeep though."

But there was no need. Ping figured

that the game was up anyway, so he might as well go back without a fight. To the ranger's astonishment the panda cub climbed into the Jeep and sat himself down in the passenger seat.

"So, you want to be driven?" laughed Mr Ho. His question was answered when the cub removed a stick of bamboo from his rucksack and stuck it into his mouth. Ping was making himself comfortable for the long trip home.

🐾

It would be a lie to say that Ping did not have several panic attacks during the journey. He was, after all, expecting a strict lecture from his mother and a

telling-off from the fat ranger. But when
he arrived back at the fat ranger's hut, he
was surprised to be greeted by a wall of
beaming faces, and as he stood up on his
seat and the faces parted, he saw a line of
cages behind them, and inside each cage
was a frightened panda cub, not so very
different in age from Ping himself.

Curious, Ping jumped down from the Jeep. His paws had barely touched the ground before he was hit from the side by a warm, furry missile. It was An.

"You're back!" she cried, hugging Ping until he could barely breathe. "I knew there was nothing to worry about. I said that the rangers would find you, didn't I, Mummy?"

"Indeed you did," laughed their mother. "Did you find what you were looking for out there?" she asked Ping quietly.

"I wasn't really looking for anything," Ping whispered in reply.

"No," said his mother. "I didn't really think you were."

After a nervous pause, Ping asked, "Aren't you going to shout at me?"

"Would you like me to?" she asked.

"No," said Ping quickly. "Not at all. But the fat ranger's going to tell me off, isn't he?"

"I very much doubt it," she said. "Do you honestly think the fat ranger would go to all this trouble to find you if all he wanted to do was tell you off?"

Ping thought about this for a moment.

"They need you, Ping, because they decided that you're the one who would be best at making our international panda friends feel at home."

I'm not sure I will, Ping thought

nervously. *Not when they get to know the real me.*

A few minutes later, the cages had all been opened, the rangers had retired to their hut and the panda cubs were sitting in a silent circle staring at each other. They had all travelled a great distance and their journeys had been very muddling for them.

Ping realised that, as the host, it was up to him to put his guests at ease, but because he'd never done it before, he didn't know where to start. He had, however, come up with a rather clever plan to keep his identity secret. He had decided that he wouldn't tell them his name unless someone specifically asked. In that way, there was a slim chance that he might avoid disappointing them.

"Welcome to Wolagong Nature Reserve," he began. "I know that this must seem strange to you, having recently lived in a zoo, but don't be scared of all the space we've got here. It doesn't bite. Well, not unless it's a snow leopard, anyway!"

One of the cubs squealed in terror. Ping's attempt at humour had made the visitors even more jumpy than before.

"It was a joke," he said quickly. "It wasn't funny. I know that. Sorry. Now, where was I? Oh yes… We want you to think of this place as home. Take a look around, chew on some of our delicious bamboo, find yourself a comfy place to sleep and in no time at all, I'm sure you'll be wondering why you ever felt anxious.

"So now I'd like to hand over to you. I thought it might be a good ice-breaker if each of you was to tell the group who you are and where you come from. OK? Let's start on my left."

"My name is Jack and I've come from London."

"Hello, Jack," said Ping, encouraging the others to join in.

"And I'm Adelaide, but you can call me Ade. And this is my friend Henry. We're from Down Under."

"Hello, Ade and Henry from Down Under."

And so it went on. By the time Viveka, Hamish, Manuel and Nattapong had introduced themselves, the panda cubs were all shaking paws and calling out each other's names with gusto.

"Great!" said Ping, standing up briskly. "You all know each other. Now you can go and explore the reserve."

"But we do not know who you are," said Nattapong. "You have not told us your name yet."

Ping froze.

"Yes, I did," he bluffed, trying not to give anything away.

"No, you didn't," cried the other seven cubs in unison.

"Oh, didn't I?" smiled Ping nervously. He looked around the circle of expectant faces and gulped. "It's… erm… Pg," he mumbled.

"Speak up, mate," shouted Ade. "I can't hear you."

"Pg," repeated Ping.

"Pig?!" exclaimed Viveka. "What kind of name is 'Pig' for a panda?"

"His name is Ping," said a voice from outside the circle. All eyes turned to see who had spoken. "And I'm his twin sister, An."

Ping's stomach flipped. He felt as sick

as a Sichuan parrot as he turned round to face the friends he had fibbed to. To his surprise, they were gazing at him in awe and wonderment, their mouths stretched upward in soppy grins.

"So *you* are the amazing Ping!" cried Jack, while Nattapong fell to his knees by Jack's side.

"Emperor of China!" he said, bowing low and scraping his nose along the ground.

"All hail the emperor!" cried the other six cubs. Then they too bowed down and touched the ground in adoration.

Although Ping was lost for words, he was sufficiently wise to know that now was not a good time to be speechless. Now was the time to speak.

"Ahem!" he said, clearing his throat and catching his worshippers' attention. "That's very kind of you. I really am most honoured… but I think I may need to explain something."

CHAPTER TEN

Ping was not expecting six of the panda cubs to stand up and applaud him. Nor was he prepared for Nattapong to raise his voice in anger.

"Silence!" he shouted, while still bowing. "This is most disrespectful! When the emperor of China says that he wants to explain something, we should listen!"

The other cubs immediately fell silent, stopped clapping and hung their heads in shame.

"You are right," said Viveka, the fabulous baker from Vienna. "We are sorry, Great Emperor Ping."

"N-no, really, there's no n-need," stammered Ping. "That's what I wanted to say…"

"The emperor is going to speak," roared Nattapong again. "Pray silence for the emperor!"

"You really must stop calling me that," exclaimed Ping. "I don't deserve the title."

"The emperor is too modest," said Hamish. "It does him much credit."

"*But I'm not the emperor!*" shouted Ping.

"Yes, you are," called out Adelaide. "Nattapong told us."

"He said that in the letter you wrote him you'd accidentally let it slip out," explained Henry. "Now you are embarrassed. We understand."

"I am embarrassed, yes," said Ping. "But not for that reason."

"I know why," Viveka called out. "It is because in your letter to me you happened to mention that you were a Winter Olympian."

The pandas gasped in admiration, while

178

Ping found himself even more tongue-tied.

"This is not what I meant to happen," he said.

"Of course not," said Hamish. "You didn't want anyone else but me to know that you were a classical bagpipe player. That's why you wrote it in my letter. Och, there's nothing wrong with letting everyone know how talented you are."

"But I'm not!" cried Ping.

"So you're telling me you're not a dragon-fighter?" scoffed Manuel. "I don't believe you. Emperors always fight dragons. It's what they do best."

"I wish you'd all just stop being nice to me," begged Ping.

"Why would you write it down if it wasn't true?" asked Nattapong.

Then suddenly, the penny dropped. One by one the pandas' expressions changed – from adoration to disbelief to disappointment.

Ping was unmasked.

"If you are not the emperor," said Nattapong, "then who are you?"

There was silence while Ping gathered his courage.

"I'm Ping," he said simply.

"The emperor's son?"

"No. I have nothing to do with the emperor," he confessed. "I'm just plain, ordinary Ping, an ordinary giant panda...

unlike all of you," he added shamefully, barely able to look at the confused faces in front of him.

"It is me who should be bowing down," he said, turning to Jack. "Look at you. A panda who has met the Queen of England and designs her blinds. It's a rare privilege to meet you, Jack."

He moved his focus of attention round the circle. "Adelaide and Henry. Cowabunga! Two pandas who can really surf. Respect, dudes." He pointed at Viveka. "A fabulous baker who makes a delicious Viennese Victoria Dundee Lemony Spongy Fruity Nutty Jammy Cupcake." He turned to the next pair of staring black eyes. "Hamish, a TV celebrity, no less, who dances the Highland fling better than anybody else on *Strictly Come Scottish Dancing*! Awa' the noo, Hamish! And the bravest of brave bullfighters…" Ping acknowledged the panda from Spain with a sweep of his arm. "Manuel," he said, bowing his head. "I salute your courage. And finally… Nattapong."

The panda cub from Thailand was still bowing down.

"You," said Ping, "who not only lead a life of goodness and quiet contemplation, are also National Thai Kick-boxing Champion… It's not right that you should bow to me. I am the one who is not worthy.

You are the guys who do the amazing stuff
while all I do is sit in this nature reserve
week in, week out, eating bamboo and

disappearing into the forest for a poo forty-seven times a day."

To be absolutely honest, Ping felt he might have gone a little bit over the top at the end, but he didn't really care. At least he'd told the truth and now he felt better – much better – as if a heavy weight had been lifted from his shoulders.

An uncomfortable silence greeted Ping's confession. As An was once heard to remark, you could have heard a Ping drop. It was not a hostile silence; it was embarrassment. Nobody quite knew what to say.

It was Ping's mother who spoke first, raising her voice above An's gentle sobbing.

"There are three types of bravery," Mao

Mao said. "*Bravery in battle, bravery in love and bravery in truth. And of these three, the most brave is bravery in truth because telling the truth strips a bear bare and leaves him nowhere to hide.*"

Then a lone voice piped up from the back.

"I think you're being rather hard on yourself, old man," it said.

To the astonishment of all, Jack stepped into the middle of the circle.

"I mean, we all knew that what you told us in your letters wasn't true, but then… maybe what we wrote back wasn't exactly true either."

Ping shook his head. What was this?

"I've never met The Queen," Jack went on. "And I've certainly never designed blinds for Buckingham Palace."

"And I can't bake for toffee," chipped in Viveka. "In fact, I hate the taste of cake. It's not a patch on bamboo."

Ping could not believe what he was hearing.

"So why did you say that you did?" he asked, realising the stupidity of his question before it had even passed his lips.

"Same reason you did," answered Adelaide.

"Haven't you ever surfed then?" he asked.

"Nope. Henry and I have never even

been to the beach."

"And I tried the Highland fling once, fell over and broke my leg," said Hamish. "That was the end of my dancing career. Thankfully."

Ping had become slightly giddy with excitement. It was as if all his worries had grown wings and were leaving his body one by one through the top of his head.

"And you, Manuel?" he ventured.

"You wouldn't catch me fighting bulls," the Spanish panda replied. "Much too dangerous."

"Nattapong, what about you?" Ping asked. "No kick-boxing?"

"Not on your life," said Nattapong.

"Why would I want to do that? It might hurt."

"And your life of calm and tranquillity?"

Nattapong shrugged. "I'm a panda, Ping. What can I say? I eat bamboo, I sleep all the time and forty-seven times a day I need a poo. If that's not calm and tranquil, what is?"

"So we're all the same?" Ping said eagerly.

"We are all the same," confirmed Nattapong. "Giant pandas through and through."

"Not entirely," said An, pushing into the circle. "I mean, Ping and I live in the wild, but you lot live in zoos."

"The young lady has a point," said Jack. "Where you live, Ping, is utterly amazing. All this space in which to have these great adventures."

"And you are so brave to live somewhere where snow leopards run free," added Hamish.

"You think I'm brave?" said Ping, smiling.

"I do," Hamish said. "Very brave. You didn't have to make up stories to impress us."

"But you are pretty bonzer at it!" laughed Adelaide. "That sure is some imagination you've got there, Ping."

"It's not just me," Ping said. "I think

we're all rather good storytellers, don't you? In fact, if there's one thing we've discovered from all this, it's that giant pandas have the best imaginations in the world and can make an adventure out of anything. We might look a bit boring, but as the old saying goes… *Never judge a book by its cover!*"

"Hear, hear," said Jack, and everyone cheered and whooped in agreement.

"Nobody knows what incredible yarns we're spinning in our heads!"

And with that, they made preparations for a giant party that night – at which all the pandas sat together in front of a roaring campfire, toasting bamboo sticks in the flames and telling each other wild and brilliant stories from around the world.

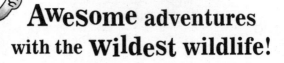

Awesome Animals

Awesome adventures with the Wildest wildlife!

OUT NOW!

Meerkat Madness
IAN WHYBROW

More Meerkat Madness
A funny furry adventure
IAN WHYBROW

Meerkat Madness Flying High
Wup wup and away!
IAN WHYBROW

Penguin Pandemonium
Little birds, big dreams
Jeanne Willis

Penguin Pandemonium
The Rescue

RACCOON RAMPAGE
HANG OUT WITH THE HOLE-IN-THE-TREE GANG!
ANDREW COPE

RACCOON RAMPAGE THE RAID
ANDREW COPE

COMING SOON!

PANDA PANIC
Watch out for the world's wildest pandas!
Running Wild
Jamie Rix